by
Suzanne Chiew

Illustrated by
Rosie Butcher

Stella and the Wishing Star

 tiger tales

Stella found a fallen star.
It was tangled in the branches
of an oak tree.

"If I rescue that star," whispered Stella,
"it will make all my wishes come true!"

Stella scrambled up the trunk and wriggled
the star free. "That tickles!" she giggled as
the star twinkled in her paws.

Wrapping a piece of string around
the star's tummy, Stella tied it to
her bike and headed home.

Suddenly, Stella heard a noise.
"Achoo!" It was Badger!
"Oh, Stella," he sighed.
"My babies can't sleep, and I have
a sore throat, so I can't sing to
them. What can I do?"

"Oh, no!" said Stella.
The star sparkled
above her head, and it
gave her an idea.

"I wish I may, I wish I might," Stella whispered, "wish for a lullaby to sweeten this night!"

In a flash, the air was filled with twinkly notes.
The baby badgers were soon sleeping softly,
but the star looked a little smaller.
"Thank you," Badger yawned.
"Sleep well and sweet dreams!"

Stella hadn't gone far when
she met Fox.
"I'm so glad to see you!" said Fox.
"My night-light just fizzled out.
I'll never get home without it."

The little star glimmered, and Stella knew just what to do. "I wish I may, I wish I might," she smiled, "light up this lantern and make it shine bright."

With a flicker, Fox's lantern sprang to life,
but the star shone a little less brightly.
"How kind you are!" beamed Fox.
"Good night, Stella."

"This is wonderful," Stella smiled.
"What will I wish for next?" But just then . . .

. . . Mole stumbled across the path
and bumped into Stella's bicycle!
   "Oof! I'm sorry, Stella!" he groaned.
"I didn't see you there. My glasses are
broken, and I can't see a thing. I wish
I could get them fixed."

"I can help," said Stella.
"Mole, give me your paw;
we'll make a wish together."

"I wish I may, I wish I might," started Stella.

"Fix my glasses and make them just right," finished Mole.

The little star flickered
and fluttered.
    "Oh!" gasped Stella.
"Will it work?"
    Then, with a twinkle
and a sparkle . . .

. . . Mole's glasses were fixed!

"They're perfect!" cheered Mole. "Thanks, Stella!" And he headed off to bed.

By now, the star was barely shining.

"Oh, star, you've been so kind," said Stella, "and now there's only enough stardust left for one last wish."

The stars above her head shimmered.
That gave Stella an idea.

"Star light, star bright," she began,
"I wish I may, with all my might, send
my friend home to the dark, starry night."

With a WHOOOOOOSH, the star soared skyward.
"Good-bye!" waved Stella. "And thank you!"